FRAGRANCE OF LIFE

Ramesh Rangan

Contents

Most persons would have seen the movie "A baby's day out" where a cute little baby outwits a gang of crooks out to kidnap it for a King's ransom. However unbelievable, the antics of the kid and it's dumb kidnappers always brings out a smile in even the most hardcore pessimist. As usual, the policemen come in at the last when all's well that ends well and the crooks get their just desserts.

The real-life scenario is totally different. If we replace the baby with a young girl just engaged, the crooks by a gaggle of shopkeepers trying their best to sell their wares to the unsuspecting kids and the policemen by the hapless parents, the story could be remarkably similar in casting. Except for one major difference. This story has a very happy ending, with complete success for the crooks, the girl beaming joyfully and the father having a wintry smile on his lips while unburdening his wallet of its contents, checking carefully whether there was enough money to pay for the cab drive back home. You see, these days, OLA and UBER cabbies prefer cash only in-spite of the facility of cashless transactions soaring in leaps and bounds.

The first stop is obviously the jewellery showroom. Their USP is offering the discount. Trust any person not to fall for this gambit. The spiel would range from reducing making charges, wastage, caratage and simple cash discounts or gifts. The buyers are so happy with the free gifts that the jewellers get away with atrociously crooked deals. For example, a cooker worth Rs.2000 at MRP is offered against jewellery purchases of Rs.40000/-. In reality, the cost price of the cooker (usually unbranded) is less than half the MRP. This amounts to 2 1/2% discount whereas the jewellery price is jacked up anywhere between 10-20% by loading wastage, making charges etc. Is it any wonder that despite the skyrocketing price of the yellow metal, every day, a new jewellery shop gets inaugurated in the commercial hub. With space being scarce in the main markets, these jewellers open shop in the suburbs. They seem to have realised, albeit late, that the hordes of cash stuffed in cupboards and quilts, are actually overflowing in these so called middle class areas. The best part is that in the TV ads, three well known film personalities recommend buying jewellery, selling the same to meet exigencies and pledging the same to raise finances, all within a period of 10 minutes of television viewing time.

The next halt, is the saree shops and dress shops which abound in any commercial district. In Chennai, the main hub is T Nagar, wherein all the main drapers and couturiers are located. Nallis, Kumarans, Pothys, RMKVs, Sundaris and many more branded outlets are located within hand-shaking distance. While competing fiercely with each other, when it comes to fooling the customers, they are in the same team. The prices of sarees is to be seen to be believed. RMKV once came up with a Kanjeevaram saree priced at Rs.50 lacs plus, with the Ramayana embroidered in Golden zari and studded with diamonds. Not that other varieties are cheap. A true-blue Kanjeevaram saree will set you back by at least Rs.1 lac. As for fashion, it is always revolving full circle. Grandma's saree designs are the rage in today's style. Temple borders have made a strong comeback as also Oosi Vaanams (vertical jari strands woven across the body of the saree in a shimmering fashion). Since gold and silver prices are way out of reach of the Mango Man, these expensive sarees now use copper zari for even the most expensive sarees. Loser? Obviously the customer. These are the expensive ones for special occasions like the Saptapadi or the Nischayathartham (betrothal). In addition, at least half a dozen designer sarees are needed for various rituals during the course of the wedding. For the grand reception, the trend for NOVIs is to wear expensive Kanjeevarams while the SOVI brides prefer lehengas. After all, dressing has no boundaries.

By this time, the hunger pangs start to bite. After all, wading through jewellery showrooms and half a dozen saree shops is excruciatingly hard work involving at least 7-8 hours each day. For similar work, MNREGA workers get about Rs.200/- per day, while the father shells out a minimum of RS.200000/- for each shift, at the minimum. There are excellent hotels and restaurants nearby catering to just such a demand. From crisp paper roasts, to fluffy idlis, full-blown puris, to a wholesome thali, it is a gourmet's dream. There are ample varieties of non-vegetarian cuisines too. Since this hub is now famous across India and even globally, restaurants catering to different cultures are available, including Burmese, Chinese, European etc. Again cross border foodies rule the roost. While the locals prefer exotic cuisine, the people from other States and countries prefer the paper dosa, not knowing whether to eat it or read the current news. The accompaniments are as spicy as the Bhut Jhalokia chilly varieties of Assam, which does cause frequent Delhi Bellies subsequently.

Having appeased the hunger pangs, the search resumes. For each saree, one needs to buy matching upper garments, with exotic embroidery. The tailors and embroiderers are specialists in their trade and while the fabric is usually a part of the saree, the stitching and embroidery charges almost match with the saree pricing. The strange fact is that the lesser fabric used in stitching the garment, the pricing goes up exponentially. Their delivery schedules are so tight that one has to wait at least a few weeks to get their appointment.

Now come the trinkets. Every girl cannot be from the Muthoot family, to be decked from top to bottom in at least 10-15 kgs of gold ornaments. To make the girls feel like real princesses, there are specialist shops catering to designer artificial jewellery, also for a price. One can buy them or even hire them for the grand event. In photo ops, they look even better than original jewellery. In fact, one shop specialises in having a perfect copy of the Kohinoor diamond. Another one has a replica of the famous (infamous?) emerald necklace of the Hyderabad Nizam. From artificial jewellery meant for dancers, this industry has come a long way indeed. With the diamond hub at Surat, also switching over to man-made diamonds, the world of precious jewellery will never be the same again. However, the bottom-line is the same: Get less value for more bucks.

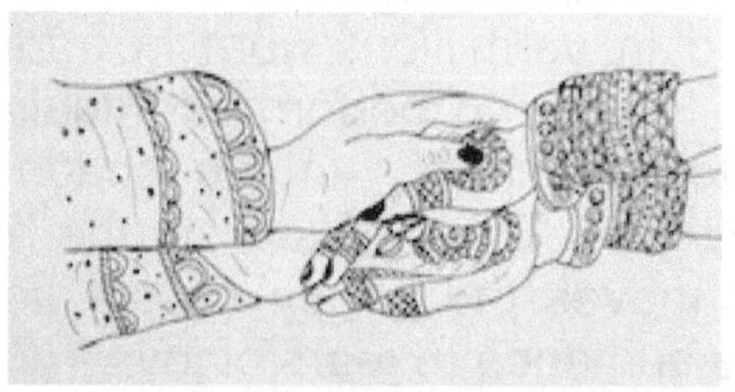

Last but not the least, are the glass bangles. It is a market in itself. Entering the narrow corridors, one could mistake it for Alladin's cave. The vivid colours, matching sets, and ability of the bangle seller to give a set for each and every colour ever seen in the world, makes it a unique experience. The seller often wears the same to showcase the beauty and allure. The prices are fairly reasonable and for once, the father regrets the fact that he could never be seen wearing such grand stuff.

In contrast, the grooms have very limited choice. Either they buy traditional suits from Raymonds in a limited range of colours or go for a pyjama kurta or at best a sherwani. In SOVI weddings, all the groom gets is a two piece cotton dhoti, dipped in vermillion, worn in traditional style. He has to perform all rituals bare chested, be it 40° in the shade or a freezing 0°. The smoke from the havan-kund moves the happy couple and the entire audience to tears of joy.

Now comes the happy part. Every parent's lifetime desire is fulfilled when their darling daughter gets a good match in life.

After all, seeing the glow of happiness in her eyes and the joyful steps she takes when selecting her choice of dresses and jewellery for the grand occasion makes every moment precious. After all, what is money but a few bits of paper or a swipe of a card. As the old Mastercard Advertisement goes: The happiness of your daughter is priceless. For everything else, there is Mastercard.

To sum up, it is every parent's desire to see their children enjoy Life to the full, filled with happiness, prosperity and good health. Both families gain a son / daughter and that is what weaving strong strands in the societal fabric is all about.

========================

Living in society, and getting immersed in our daily routines, we hardly ever recognise the persons who help us unobtrusively in going through life smoothly. These are the elves, the worker ants who keep the wheels of society well-oiled and fit. Observing these persons moving about their daily lives is an interesting subject in itself. One never realises that Life never deals out the same hand of cards to everyone. From being born with the proverbial golden spoon in the mouth to being born in parts of the world where even bare necessities are a daily struggle, each and every individual's life is unique. The difference is made by what one makes out of his or her Life with the best possible use of available opportunities and resources. In this world, there are no second chances. While the stars and superstars shine brightly (mostly undeservedly too) and corner all the attention in a world full of persons starved of role models, it is the daily workers around us who go about their tasks without any expectations, who really deserve attention.

This is not an exhaustive list of all such people around us. These, then, are the ordinary people who facilitate our daily routines. Normally, we never notice them and treat them as if they didn’t exist. It is only when they do not come that we find how important they are in our lives. Imagine having to clear wet stinking domestic garbage, wear un-pressed clothes, miss breakfast or having a house full of clutter awaiting disposal. These persons bear untold hardships and yet they carry their burdens cheerfully. From paying a cut to the local strongman, the beat policeman or the occasional petty thief, they still manage to smile at life's bouncers. They cry to make us happy and laugh when they are nervous. They fight for what they believe in. They stand up to injustice. They don't take "no" for an answer when they believe there is a better solution. They go the extra mile so their family can have a better Life. One of the above mentioned persons is educating an orphaned girl child despite her own earnings being pitifully small. An introspection may reveal that at least in terms of kind heartedness, they are as good if not better than many others. The least one can do is to recognise each one as an individual, with a respectable place in society. Every one of these persons has a family and for the spouse and their children, this family is a microcosm of the cozy world they live in.

These are the heroes and heroines in Real Life. Reams and reams are written about valiant soldiers who die on the frontline, and more money is made in filming their life stories with the REEL heroes raking in astronomical sums, while the producers laugh all the way to the Bank. Film stars are fawned upon mindlessly because the average individual does not accept the reality that these are but human beings just like the common citizen. A brief description of our day-to-day heroes and heroines is given in the next few paragraphs

Being the festival season, what better way to honour such unsung personalities than to appreciate their contribution. A sample list of our day-to-day support system comprising of common persons is described, without whom organised society would have been destroyed aeons ago.

There is an old lady, let's call her Chellatha, nearing 50, looking all of 70, crushed down by the burden of living. Well before the legal age, she stepped into married life with stars in her eyes. Her husband turned out to be a good-for-nothing lout and after gifting her with an unborn baby (probably the only gift he gave his wife in their Life), he simply vanished. The baby also turned out to be differently abled with poorly developed abilities because of the mother's poor health. This special child is now nearing 35 years and the mother takes care of her with tender loving care. She earns a pittance by working in a few homes, by adorning their doorsteps with beautiful rangolis, which is considered highly auspicious. Her cheer and smile perks up the entire household. Her greetings are most sought after and seeing her early in the morning is considered to be a blessing in itself. She imbues a golden hue in all her personal interactions.

Have we ever given a thought to how and where the garbage we create thoughtlessly at home gets disposed of?

Even today, almost everyone sweeps their house spotlessly clean and throws the muck in front of the road or street. Enter the conservancy worker Maran, a young individual, who gives a call in all households at the break of dawn to collect the refuse and garbage which the privileged accumulate over the previous day. His ways of guiding these individuals on segregation of waste products would do any text-book armchair expert on waste management proud. He also keeps track of the well-being of individual members in the household. His cheerful demeanour has endeared him to the mamis and mamas of the neighbourhood and even a day's absence is keenly missed. What a great lesson we have learnt from this humble worker.

What a strange moniker for the first hawker to hit the lanes and by-lanes of the bustling locality is the vendor of leafy greens.

For most households, a dish made from greens is almost mandatory. It has the reputation for being full of fibre and one of the healthiest foods in a vegetarian platter. No one ever asks her name and almost everyone knows her by the moniker "Amma Keerai ", which means leafy greens. The lady would be in her mid-fifties and had probably forgotten her own name. The locality has a healthy mix of Gujaratis and Rajasthanis also and when they call out to the lady in their dialect, the lilting accents would melt God's heart.

Her basket contains almost all types of routine greens, besides many exotic varieties. Her marketing skills are amazing, since she prescribes and provides certain greens to cure daily problems like joint pains, constipation, etc. It is a proven fact that many such daily health problems do get sorted out by the treatment. Had she the opportunity to education, she could have been an Internist of repute.

For the lazy homemakers and even more lazy bachelors and spinsters, the moving vendor of tiffin items is the answer to a prayer. Clad in spotless white dhoti and shirt, Murugan gets homemade idlis, vada and idiyappam (a sort of noodles made from fresh rice dough) accompanied by delicious chutneys and sambar. On occasions when he gets delayed, he is literally mobbed by his regular customers. His USP is freshness of the merchandise cooked at home.

Almost always, his stock gets exhausted very fast and the demand for his services is perennial. It is pertinent to note that the Swiggys and Zomatos indulge in similar activities and keep losing hundreds of crores each year, while Murugan takes home a profit each day. Maybe these aggregators could benefit from the innovative strategies of such vendors. In keeping with times, he proudly displays his unique QR Code and accepts UPI payments.

MOHAN: TOUGH COP TO VENDOR OF TENDER COCONUTS

In these days of health consciousness, most people prefer a healthy drink of coconut water after breakfast, to the traditional Kaapi. Enter Mohan, an ex-cop turned vendor of tender coconut water. Usually clad in a lungi, in 50 shades of grey (pun intended), and armed with a sharp cleaver, he slices the top of the tender coconut with a single chop, punches a hole and offers it to his customers with a straw and a flourish. One could almost imagine how he would have treated the wretches whom he had arrested in his previous role. With another deft cut, he splits open the now empty shell out the deliciously sweet pulp for his customers. The taste would definitely match the best of desserts offered in any star rated eatery. His QR code is stuck on a healthy and round tender coconut, serving as an advertisement for both his wares and the UPI Service Provider.

Can the mornings in any household begin without an offering of flowers to the family deity? Enter Poovamma, about whom a reference has been made earlier in a different story. Her basket, full of closely strung jasmines, mogras, yellow chrysanthemums and roses is a beautiful sight to behold. With her customers being regulars, no marketing is required. One wonders if fate had been more kind, she could have been an international economist. Looking at the width or gap in her flower strands, one could visualise whether the flower bazaar was bullish or bearish.

Ever since the onslaught of Covid hit the citizens with a sledgehammer, the Government health authorities have engaged persons to keep a weekly check on the health of its citizens, especially the golden oldies (I mean senior citizens). The blue uniformed worker Sarada, diligently calls on each household and records the vital parameters of the citizens.

Any abnormal symptoms get promptly reported and a trained health worker is at your doorstep. While it's a nice feeling to be pampered, these intrusions on one's privacy could often give one the blues. Poorly paid, and that too erratically, these workers deserve a cup of coffee or tea, to help relieve them from their thankless task.

Bahadur, who claims to work as a night watchman in the colony is visible only once a month to claim his monthly salary of Rs.10 from each household. One can only imagine what sort of work he would be doing at night for this pittance. For the locals, he is GOORGA (Gurkha is the local slang for any watchman). A perfect caricature of the watchman in the movie 3 Idiots, probably calling out AAAL EES WELL, no one has seen him other than on collection day. However, one must admit that his absence or delayed visits for collecting money, cause some concern, for his well-being, as he must be not a day short of 80. Knowing fully well that this self-appointed watchman cannot allow one to lower one's guard, he is usually indulged in because of the comic interlude of his presence itself.

How could one forget the traditional rickshaw puller Rasesh? Having started off pulling the hand rickshaw, gradually upgraded to a cycle rickshaw and eventually fitted with a motor, he has seen them all. From the beginning, he apparently had a fondness for dabbling in workers' rights. His rickshaw always has a photo of a bearded person whom none could recognise.

Upon asking, he claimed it was of Siguvaara, who was a labour leader from the ruling party. With great difficulty , one could make out that it bore a very faint resemblance to Che Guevara. He refused to accept any such explanation and continues to ply his trade with the red board stuck on his rickshaw. In the South, political affiliations run deep and one wouldn't be surprised if he remains the sole representative of Communism on Judgement Day.

KASI: THE VENDOR OF "GOOD LUCK" BRAND SALT

If it is a Friday, Kasi, the seller of rock salt appears promptly. In Tamilnadu, there is a firm belief that buying salt on a Friday brings prosperity, whether one needs it or not. In fact, buying salt is considered better than buying gold and it's an affordable option too. Kasi the vendor, enjoys this belief as it is a lifeline for him. In many households, one can find tins of rock salt accumulated through Friday purchases. It is also used along with red chillies, to cast off the evil eye. On festive occasions, especially the Car festival in the temple, this salt is poured under the chariot's wheels.

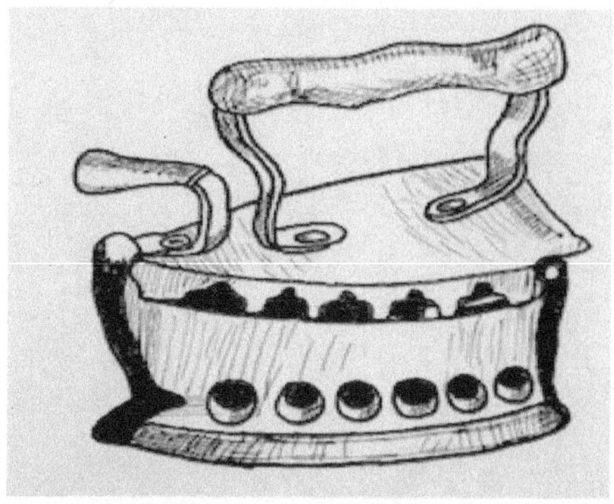

Vadivel, the owner of a moving laundry, is another regular, whose absence is keenly felt. Using a brass iron box, heated with charcoal, he helps all the locals to dress up in well pressed garments. His rates are quite reasonable too. His only flaw is his unpredictability. He is a most valued customer of Tasmac, the government owned speakeasy. Whenever he needs money for a session, his Laundry activities are at a peak. To his credit, he is extremely well behaved at work.

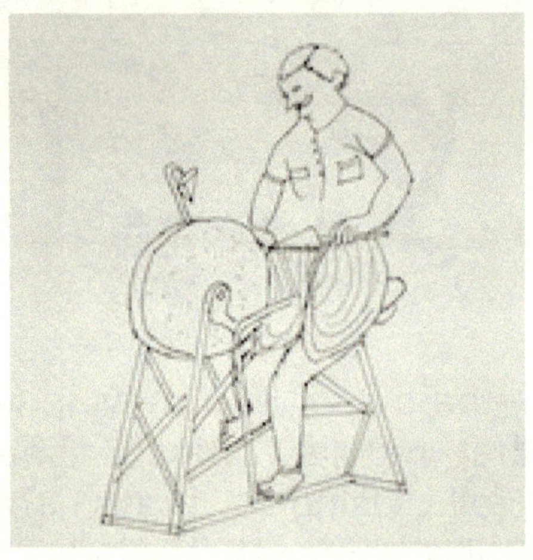

Another unusual vendor is Venky , the cutler or professional knife sharpener. Twice a week, he makes his rounds, displaying a dazzling array of sharp knives for sale in addition to his grinding wheel. In most households today, it is the man of the house who does the chopping. Venky is in great demand for his skills. To find him hemmed in by a few ladies with cutting instruments of various shapes, waiting to get them sharpened, is a sight to behold. The men peep in carefully trying to ascertain if their spouse is buying any new knife, for such weapons could be a double-edged sword in any domestic quarrel. With newspaper headlines screaming about giving new weapons to Ukraine to resist Russia, the palpable fear of arming the lady of the house with improved weaponry is keenly felt. As they euphemistically say, till Venky leaves, "the atmosphere was so thick that it could be cut with a knife".

Anbu, the benign buyer of anything discarded, from newspapers to plastic, steel and old broken equipment, is one of the favourites. Picking up such items for a song, he trades them in the junk market, and makes a clear profit. He has a team of workers who also engage in deep cleaning homes, water tanks, etc. He has a sister, who is a decent tailor and offers tailoring at one's doorstep. He has thus created a set-up under one roof, a smaller but more dependable version of Urban Clap and their ilk, at vastly competitive rates.

All Banks have a great customer service department to solve all problems of customers. A few examples, (all imagined but feasible) came to my mind.

Complainant: C
Customer Service department: D

C: The Passbook printer doesn't work most of the time.
D: The printer is on the verge of retirement. We have advertised for new recruits to join. (Got confused between man and machine?)

C: If we have to draw cash from ATM our self, print our own passbook and do most transactions on-line, including opening accounts, what are your staff branch doing?

D: Sometimes, we also wonder about this. (An honest answer, if there was one)

C: Why do I need to pay charges when I am depositing my own cash in my own account?

D: Do you know the risk of handling dirty currency? You should be thankful that we accept your dirty currency without protest.

C: Whenever I enter a branch, the staff are either having tea / coffee or lunch. I have to wait indefinitely.

D: As a customer satisfaction measure, we have issued instructions that the lunch / tea / tiffin is shared with all customers who are waiting. We have called it "Happy Hour Banking"

C: The Manager / staff are always busy selling loans, insurance, mutual funds, etc / enrolling Aadhar. When I need to open a simple account, I'm told it will take 4-5 days

D: In today's market, opening and closing accounts has been deleted from the definition of Banking Activity. As such, opening accounts will be done at our convenience. Regret the inconvenience.

C: Your Branch Manager and other staff know nothing about the rules and regulations regarding their job.

D: Psstt. No one in Head Office knows them either. You should refer to Reserve Bank Master Circulars to know something.

C: Why does every employee sitting in the counter looks like he or she is suffering from either headaches or constipation?

D: Please look at the mirror placed in the lobby to know the reason.

GOLDEN OLDIE

To twist an old song from Sound of Music:

I am 66, going on 67,
Oldies I'm ready for a break,
Fellows I meet

Will tell me I repeat
'bout those glorious bygone days.
I am 66, going on 67,
Devious as ever,
Casting glances
At grannies and aunties,
'cause others are out of range

Serving the mistress, Day and night,
Working harder than ever,
Floating memories of days gone by
Which are now lost forever.

Trying to find myself again,
In this ruthless world of men,
Dreaming of the days when, in future,
I will be young again

Siesta broken, reality hit me
At 67, life is not forever,
Enjoying each day with friends and family,
Is the only way to go into the wild blue yonder

=====================

Nuts and Veda, the evergreen quintessential Tambram couple, had just emerged from a hectic year. The year 2023 had begun on a high note with the engagement of their daughter. An arranged wedding, if ever there was one, the preparations had taken place at a hectic pace. The wedding went off in a blur of activity, most of which they could barely remember. Looking at the wedding albums, they saw themselves figuring in strange rituals, which they never recollected having ever performed.

In South India, the wedding is but a prelude to the social obligations to be performed during each festival which follows. One festival merged into another and each was celebrated with gusto, in which the piece-de-resistance was invariably a grand menu. After attending meticulously to all their duties and obligations and eating so many goodies, both Nuts and Veda were too tired to take care of themselves either through exercise or walks. Result: a healthy increase in the middle and lower portions of the anatomy, especially the gluteus maximus.

Good habits are hard to form but bad habits tend to accumulate quickly. With very little motivation to prepare homely meals, the couple were frequenting the eateries in and around their area. One evening Nuts and Veda went into their favourite restaurant for dinner. Being favored clients, they were immediately recognised and given a special table, bypassing the long waiting list of hungry diners.

As chance would have it, the adjacent table was filled with a big gathering. One could easily make out that it was two families meeting each other probably for the first time, in a formal manner. The men on either side were remarkably quiet while the ladies, three on each side, were overtly garrulous. When shaking their heads expressively, the diamonds in their earrings, necklaces and rings sparkled away to glory, bedazzling the casual glances cast in their direction. The sides were evenly matched both in couture and demeanor.

Now, Nuts was as inquisitive as the person next door and being a banker, had developed the habit of hearing snippets of conversation, building upon them with a fertile imagination and often coming up with the correct hypothesis. Like a well trained Dobermann, his acute sense of hearing and sight was focused and directed sharply towards the next table. From the snippets of conversation, he could make out that one group was based in Chennai and the other group was from Mangalore.

The conversation swirled around tentatively with the ladies trying to get information on each other's families. Long chains of their individual family trees were recollected and it stopped only when some common ancestor or acquaintance was identified. From there it switched on to the hectic life in Chennai versus the relaxed pace in Mangalore. It seems even the trains and planes coming into Chennai were superfast, while trains in Mangalore ambled along in keeping with the local traditions. The rambling conversation drifted inevitably to the sarees and jewellery worn for the occasion. The ladies exchanged addresses of the saree and jewellery shops, and agreed to visit these at the earliest opportunity. Nuts could imagine the husbands squirming away, not knowing how and where from to fund such an extravaganza. The group from Chennai was then joined by a lady, probably in the late thirties and the Mangalorean group by a gentleman in the same age group. They were quite unassuming in their attitudes. Sitting

quietly, their conversation, in soft tones, would have been inaudible to even the person sitting next to them.
The general conversation then switched on smoothly to the careers of their children. One of the ladies in the Chennai group was speaking about the exploits of her daughter, who was placed in a multinational firm after a brilliant academic career. A lady from the Mangalore group spoke about her son having completed his Masters in Surgery and was presently in that hallowed country USA.

Nuts' imagination started to soar. He immediately guessed that this was a semi-formal boy meets girl party, with an alliance in the offing. However, to his disappointment, he could neither see the prospective boy or girl, who were the topic of discussion. Taking a look at the boy's mother, he guessed her to be the master of the house, who would run her home as a school hostel warden. In contrast, his take on the nature of the girl's mother was that of a soft person, well versed in running the household seamlessly. In his imagination, he saw a lavish destination wedding being celebrated. He imagined the day when the new bride would enter the domain of her mother-in-law and get bruised with the clash of egos. He consoled himself that this would be but for a short time as the girl would eventually move on to the Dreamland called USA with the good doctor in tow. (Or is it the other way around?)

He was sharing all these thoughts with Veda. Having her feet firmly on the ground, Veda told Nuts to come back to reality since they didn't even know if the families had gathered there for discussing an alliance, and if so, had decided to go ahead. In any case, it was none of their business. Nuts refused to be cowed down since he had already decided in his mind, that this was a match made in heaven, decided in Woodlands (hotel) and executed in Mahabalipuram.

A few weeks later, Nuts and Veda were on their early morning visit to the temple. Traditionally, weddings are performed in the temple precincts and the day being an auspicious one, two such weddings were in progress. A flash of sunlight reflected from sparkling jewellery caught the eyes of the couple. The wedding guests seemed vaguely familiar as were the bride and groom. Veda, being a lady and blessed with an elephantine memory in the sartorial arts, was the first to recall that these were the very same guests who were dining in the adjacent table in their favourite restaurant a few weeks ago. The bride and groom were the silent couple, who had been too engrossed in talking to each other, while their relatives, on either side were trying to ascertain details of their families.

Nuts realised immediately that his guesswork had misfired badly. Veda was grinning to see him squirm. As they were passing through after peeping into the ceremony, looking at their age and traditional dress, the priest handed them akshatha (rice mixed with haldi) to shower on the couple as blessings. Happy to do so, Nuts and Veda, blessed them silently for a happy life ahead.

Going into the temple, they also recited a special prayer for the couple, whom they never knew or would never know.

The incident taught the couple one important lesson. Humanity is a complex chain and one never knows who or what is linked. Who ever said "CURIOSITY KILLED THE CAT"? In the case of Nuts and Veda, it created a lasting impression.

==============================

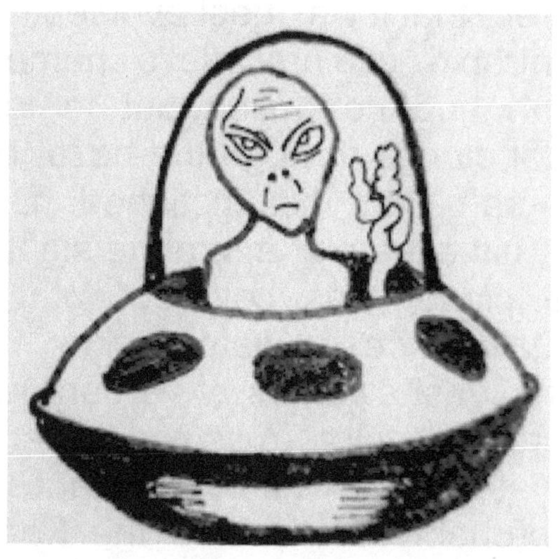

Planet Earth was being inspected by a number of alien spacecraft from the neighbouring planets. They were all looking for a planet with a hospitable environment for housing their burgeoning population, which was bursting at the seams. The natural resources in these planets had been rapaciously exploited and survival was becoming extremely tough. The only option was to find a neighbouring planet for moving out.

It wasn't as if they were unaware of Planet Earth. However, it's impenetrable atmosphere, shrouded in toxic gases and extremely hot temperatures told these explorers that it was best avoided. Once, an intrepid explorer (let's name him Boggle) had no option but to take a suicidal plunge through the haze, as his spacecraft had malfunctioned. Drifting down, his eyes met a strange sight. The entire planet was covered with huge mountains, fresh water lakes, great oceans, vast swathes of verdant jungle, wild orchards full of fruits and flowers and a climate which was so ambient that it was probably better than the Paradise which was promised by the religious seers in their own planet. The spacecraft had landed in a beautiful garden. An automatic cloak of invisibility immediately enveloped the same, which made it and it's occupant invincible too.

It was time to explore. With advanced technology, Boggle could travel across the globe at the speed of thought. What he found was way beyond imagination. The entire world was divided into a number of nations, each ruled by different species of living beings. One of the biggest nations was called the Union of States. The various provinces therein were neither united nor having any common purpose. It was ruled presently by a team of jackasses. Their main rivals were a team of elephants, who were waiting for a chance to overturn the ruling party. The strange thing was that the elephant party was led by a jackass while the party of jackasses was led by an extinct elephant (a woolly mammoth in thoughts and actions). An opportunity (called elections) was given to each citizen of the country to (s)elect their leader. This system was called 'democrazy'. A number of nations had adopted this method.

In another big country called Himdesh, democrazy had peaked. As a result, there were more groups of wannabe rulers than the electorate. The aspiring candidates ranged from all types of bovines like cows, horses, buffaloes, goats etc to even frogs in the local swamp. In fact, this nation had every type of animal dreaming of capturing power in the elections. Sensing a great opportunity quite some time back, a group of powerful Royal Tigers had taken upon themselves the task of winning over the nation and establishing order.

A third big nation was Chane, where might was right. It's citizens were quite docile and willing to believe that a single point power centre was the best thing to happen to them. The animals ranging from pigs, pandas, tigers and domestic animals, to even the inhabitants of the sea believed in this philosophy. This Nation was perennially looking forward to expanding its footprints across other nations, both in terms of power and territories.

Another country which was a huge conglomeration of Nations in the past, had been split asunder and the bits and pieces became unruly kingdoms. Unable to bear this ignominy, the rulers, led by a huge army of jackals, was busy attempting to rebuild their original frontiers. As a result, the entire planet was perpetually engaged into wars of a brutal kind.

A fifth huge landmass had never seen any type of organized administration. It consisted of small territories governed only by the principle " Might is right". The scenario was utterly confusing with cheetahs, wild dogs, jackals, foxes, tigers, rhinos, hippos, et al ruling small pieces of territories. They usually devoured each other for sustenance. The larger nations would side with one or the other ruler, simply to exploit the natural resources available.

This entire planet was governed by an umbrella organisation aptly named Union of Nations. Each country was represented by one animal. The resultant cacophony cannot be described in words. When Boggle decided to peep in, his eardrums were almost shattered by the noise levels. He beat a hasty retreat. As can well be imagined, such a mighty organisation was reduced to making loud noises on inane subjects and was effectively ineffective in implementation of any decision, big or small.

Boggle was intrigued. He had been briefed that this world was inhabited by a species called homo-sapiens (humans), who possessed great intelligence, by virtue of which, they were mighty rulers of all that was in their control. However, all he could see were various animals in positions of power. Finding a wise eagle, he made himself visible and got down to understanding the dynamics of Planet Earth. The eagle, who was witness to the changes over the eons, began briefing Boggle appropriately.

The Earth was indeed the abode of humans in the past. Their Glory reached unimaginable heights and they were virtually unchallenged. They had grown utterly complacent and began exploiting the natural resources recklessly. Carbon Fossil fuels were completely exhausted. Nuclear power residues became totally unmanageable. Mother Earth couldn't bear the torture being inflicted on her bosom. Her body heaved with disastrous consequences. Storms, floods, unbearable heat, volcanoes and diseases erupted across the world. Almost all humans were impacted and failed to survive. A thick poisonous cloud mushroomed in the atmosphere. The humans couldn't breathe and simply collapsed and died. The animals, who were relatively living sheltered lives in the zoos of the world, managed to survive this apocalypse.

Over time, as exploitation of the resources stopped, Mother Earth reclaimed what was hers by right. The jungles became resplendent once again, waters began sustaining life and the air, cleansed of its poisonous pollutants, became sweet again, birds chirped happily and the inhabitants of the lakes, rivers and seas were dancing away to glory. The animals had displayed remarkable resilience in survival and came back to occupy their rightful place on Planet Earth. The humans were completely eliminated. As animals evolved, they had memories of the readymade infrastructure created by humans. As it was easy to adopt a well tried system, the present world order was created. It was quite functional, with animals ruling the roost. Food become abundant again.

The animals had discovered that a few specimens of human beings had survived the disasters. They were found in remote uninhabited areas. In view of the very few survivors among humans, the animals thought of a way to preserve these specimens for their future generations to see.

They created zoos to house these humans. Since humans were a tasty delicacy for animals, it became important for the rulers of the animal kingdom to protect humans from Animal Man conflicts. Strict rules were made protecting humans from being killed recklessly. Human corridors were created for their safety.

Transgressions were severely punished. Since human bones were ideal for crafting artefacts, killing them for their bones was banned. However, a few countries continued to breed human beings on a commercial scale, thus spawning a global trade in such products, albeit illegal.

Boggle was now equipped with priceless knowledge. He became the repository of all knowledge that could lead to the destruction and fall of a civilization. It was at this stage that Boggle decided to monetize this knowledge. For a good price and knowing that the information was entirely in his control, Boggle managed to amass incalculable wealth in the Universe of Nations. In the end, all things remained the same, with only the order of players being reversed.

You may be wondering as to the reasons for writing this piece in reverse mode. Yours truly was travelling in a train with the seats facing in the opposite direction of travel. As such, the thoughts also got reversed as in a dream and got converted into words. On waking up, realisation dawned that the scenario was no so far-fetched. If humans do not stop their plundering of natural resources and remain selfish, forgetting future generations, there may come a day when there is no future or a future generation in this planet. The moot question is: Is anyone listening?

==========================

In the placid life of a retired banker and his wife, excitement was a rare commodity. Their calm life was like a temple pond, with rarely a ripple. Like children casting a pebble which caused ripples in the waters, the occasional excitement was provided by visits of their daughter / son and their grandchildren. As time flew by, the visits were as rare as ice in the desert. The other sources of activity included attending family functions like weddings, haldi ceremonies, first birthdays, 60th / 80th birthdays, etc. In most such functions, the couple, young at heart forever, suddenly started feeling old as they were conferred with the honourable title of "Family Elders".

Nuts and Veda were attending the wedding of a close family friend's son. The casual observation of the groom's father " now, I am a free man" when his son was tying the sacred three knots with the Mangalsutra around his doe-eyed bride, brought forth a rush of thoughts. The priest was pontificating on the significance of kanyadaan in the wedding to an uninterested audience indulging in loud chatter, in the background of the even louder notes of the nagaswaram. Nuts and Veda, who had themselves given away their daughter in Kanyadaan, were surprised that the father of the groom, for whom this wedding would bring an additional member into the family fold, should harbour such feelings. He explained that symbolically, the remote control which was supposed to be in the hands of the father, was now passed on to the bride. He explained his firm belief that while the groom tied the sacred knots, he was symbolically tying himself into a complex web of knots, impossible to untangle. Now, the task of moulding her husband was being taken up by the wife.

Nuts started thinking about his own life. From a sheltered and studious boy, an ill-tempered brat and a chance banker (Goddess Saraswati must have written his entrance exam to help him out), his marriage changed his life completely. Veda was an apparently docile girl, who in her quiet manner, completely morphed his approach to life. He became a meek(y) mouse at home and a roaring superior in office. Since management always needs someone who can be tough and tackle several bulls by their horns or whatever, his career graph was reasonably good. As luck would have it, this success was also attributed to his wife, who became his lucky mascot. He often thought about his parents who seemed to have also happily surrendered to his wife's charms, without any such feelings of loss of control. Realisation dawned that Life is but a continuum of knots, some tied by individuals, some tied by society and some by mysterious forces in the celestial world, from which there is no escape. The knots bring happiness, joy, troubles, misery and challenges in equal measure, and how one tackles the situation makes or breaks our lives.

It is said that the fastest thing in the world is the speed of light. However, human thoughts attain far greater speed and also jump trajectory in completely unrelated directions. Nuts began thinking: What is Life without Love? What is Love without relationships? What is relationship without individuality? Each living being has a unique personality within society. However, the old saying "Familiarity breeds Contempt" is all pervasive. One never values anything which is always accessible. The only exception is probably wealth which goads one to accumulate, knowing fully well that it is of no use in the afterlife, if there ever was one.

Nuts and Veda had always been living with the elders in a big family. Like any normal family, the joys, sorrows and bickerings were a part of daily routines. It didn't affect any individual materially. The children, whose mischief was quite intolerable, would create havoc in the daily routines of the elders' puja and siesta times. A mouthful of scoldings and the occasional slaps were bestowed liberally on these brats. However, to the utmost surprise, the children, instead of moving away from these elders, were more fond of them, often making the parents almost jealous. It was a lifeline which these kids threw at the elders during their twilight years and prolonged their health and relieved them from the aches and pains associated with age. Nuts and Veda barely noticed all this till one day, the elders were no more. The loss of emotional support was felt overwhelmingly and the kids seemed to have suddenly grown up. Both realised that we appreciate things only when we do not have them with us anymore. This was a strange dimension of Love and the emotions attached to it flowing from unknown springs.

Nuts and Veda used to visit various temples too, as was customary. Visiting a world famous temple in South India, with their mother, who was not in very good health, it was just a routine visit. But fate had something else in store. This temple visit was his mother's last outing. Almost after a decade, when Nuts and Veda, now all alone, went to the temple again, memories came flooding back. With moistened eyes and heavy hearts, they paid obeisance, all the while remembering their mother, who had decided to merge with the sublime and whose cherished values had become invaluable. They realised that Love transcends all boundaries and serves as a bridge between past, present and future generations. It was a wake-up call to live each day completely.

Veda was used to keeping her house spic and span with nary a thing out of place. The house was a model of good living, an example of total perfectionism. However, she had failed miserably in inculcating these habits in her daughter. As befitting a teenager, she was at her best in keeping her room always looking as if a tornado had just struck the place. Veda had become completely exhausted in trying to make her daughter understand the virtues of good housekeeping. When her daughter got married, Veda was sure that she wouldn't be able to cope with the huge tasks associated with making a house into a home. There were occasional calls to Veda from her daughter on cooking tips but for the most part, there were no major complaints from her side. After a few months, Nuts and Veda visited their daughter. Veda was shocked to see that the house was perfect in all respects and her daughter could whip up a tasty meal without any difficulty. The height of irony was that her daughter scolded Veda when she just dropped some clothes in a corner. Veda realised that her daughter was a keen observer and had absorbed all the learnings but had never practised it at home.

The story doesn't end here. When her daughter came home for the holidays, she went back to her pre-wedding habits of living like a gypsy, and always keeping her room in a mess. Veda couldn't understand this dual behaviour and burst out at her daughter. She had a simple answer: " If I can't be myself in my mother's place, where else can I do so"? This was another dimension which showed that children can let their hair down and be themselves with their parents, with the familiarity and comfort which only unconditional Love can give. After seeing off their daughter and setting her room back in order, a strange feeling overcame them: "When will she come back to create the mess again"?

Through years of having seen Life, Nuts and Veda had realised that Love is multidimensional. Parental love of their children, duly reciprocated, is the initial building block of a family. In youth, one finds Love in enjoying Life's surprises. Physical love with a spouse gets transformed into emotional Love over a period of time. Love of near and dear ones helps build strong bonds with the extended family and creates the fabric of society. Intricate designs in this fabric of Love are woven by strong friendships, which last throughout our lives. In short, Love is all pervasive and is present in every breath one takes. Looking back, Nuts and Veda had realised that though they had occasionally stumbled up blind alleys, they had managed to maintain their Life's garden, reasonably well and had managed to harvest and share the fruits and flowers with one and all. With such pleasant thoughts in their mind, they went back to sleep to face another day positively, with all its surprises and twists.

==============================

Have we ever wondered why we always do things or act in certain ways subconsciously. With WhatsApp University in full flow, such trivia is flowing like a river in spate. What are rational symbolic dams in front of such tremendous flow of utter nonsense?

We have all heard of the South African president who was famous for his witticisms. One of his favorites was on the use of the bath towel. Giving the towel a mind of its own, he used to quip that unless one is careful, the portion which wiped one's face today would also wipe one's backsides the next day, thus completing it's revenge.

Surprisingly, I came to learn that Goddess Lakshmi has two incarnations, one bringing in prosperity and the other taking it away. While the former always enters the soul from the front, the latter enters the soul surreptitiously from the back. Therefore , after a bath, one must wipe the back first to shut the backdoor entrance to negative forces. A bit like the former belief but diametrically opposite.

Sir Appleby (Permanent Secretary to James Hacker, in Yes Minister) caught on accountability for a blunder committed as a junior 30 years back causing a huge loss to the exchequer.

"The identity of this official whose alleged responsibility for this hypothetical oversight has been the subject of recent speculation is not shrouded in quite such impenetrable insecurity as certain previous disclosures may have led you to assume, and, in fact, not to put too fine a point on it, the individual in question was, it may surprise you to learn, the one to whom your present interlocutor is in the habit of identifying by means of the perpendicular pronoun."

Hacker : I beg your pardon?

Sir Humphrey after an anguished pause, "It was I".

Can our own SBI be far behind in the perpetuation of humor in office? A few incidents, across the career spectrum, and vouched for by many colleagues, are narrated below:

The Bank was an aggregation of complex kingdoms, aptly named Circles, probably because most officials were going round and round aimlessly, since the notes or proposals they were handling mostly had no beginning or end. Each kingdom had a king, who ruled eccentrically for a couple of years before moving on to a more senior (not necessarily important) role or faded away into oblivion called retirement. The courtiers and hangers on would have put to shame any of the Imperial Courts of the Mughal or British monarchs.

As the famous song in the Sound of Music starts with " Let's start at the very beginning......", the career of all new recruits in the Bank, before getting a letter of appointment, began by undergoing a medical test. What would you know but that the roly poly Bank's doctor, aptly named Doctor Doctor (for that was his name), would call the candidate into his examination room and ask him to strip, turn around and cough. God knows what his diagnosis was but it left the candidates coming out, with egos shattered, and wondering as to how banking was different from a strip tease.

The State Bank is a great leveller at all phases in the hierarchy. At the initiation stage, after a decent treatment during initial training, the candidates were given postings in the weirdest of places, mostly in rural areas with barely any road or rail access. The branches of SBI in the past were located where even devils feared to tread. Basic amenities were mostly a pipe dream. Since SBI was a Government Bank, they usually shared spaces adjacent to decrepit Government offices or rundown Government schools. The toilet was secured under lock and key which would be in the joint custody of the local official and our Branch Manager (BM). No strong room was guarded with such zeal.

Horror stories abound of branches with creepy crawlies and snakes resting cosily in strong rooms and under thick dusty ancient ledgers, which could not be destroyed. Finding these to be occupying spaces, a bright official at Head Office came up with the idea of destroying them. To save himself from any future accusations, he instructed that a copy of each book destroyed may be kept safely for future reference. So much for bureaucracy. The saving grace was the respect and awe in which the Bank staff were held because they were the custodians of money. In many centres, the BM was at the top of the social hierarchy and was a confidant to all the local families in solving their personal matters.

Talking of levelling the playing field, the BM was the monarch of all he / she surveyed in his / her domain. However, in the eyes of the Controller, the BM was but a mosquito, waiting to be swatted. This analogy extended right up to the uppermost echelons of governance. In the Corporate Office, persons who had struggled and fought hard and became successful in the rat race, often had to share room space as there were not adequate tables and chairs. It only went to prove the old adage: In a rat race, the eventual winner is also a rat.

Those days, the BM was the prisoner who was thrown to the Circus Lions. Many bosses also treated them as donkeys and used the carrot (good confidential reports) and stick (transfer to the nether world) policy to good effect. If one emerged unscathed, then he / she was deemed to be capable of shouldering higher responsibilities. On the other hand, the lucky officials manning various desks in the aptly named Controlling Office were demigods. For every poor BM, there were at least a dozen puppeteers sitting in control. Approvals for everything was required to be obtained from these individuals. Short of seeking permission to take a washroom break, the BM's life was under their total control. However the BMs were not as helpless as it seemed. With telephone connections being patchy, the BM could mostly avoid pesky calls by pretending that the connection was not going through.

The successful BM was one who could integrate his / her persona with the local milieu. While wearing formals would be the norm in Metropolitan cities, doing so in a rural area would quickly alienate the customers who could get overawed. Learning the local lingo especially for those from other parts of the country, was another weapon for success. Breaking bread with staff, meeting village elders over a cup of tea and easy approachability also facilitated their task.

How can one forget the mandatory certification required to be obtained from the Indian Institute of Bankers (IIB)? Consisting of two parts and a dozen papers, it was one of the toughest examinations to get through. In case one got it wrong, the exams did nothing to enhance the official's knowledge. The obtention of marks was a matter of pure chance. It was reputed that the office boy at IIB was given two rubber stamps marked Pass and Fail. Depending on the weight of the answer sheets, he would stamp them accordingly. Many candidates with distinction in Economics, English and Chartered Accountants were mortified to see that they had failed in their area of specialization. There are quite a few of these individuals who decided not to write the same deeming it to be below their dignity. They usually preferred to choose greener pastures to fulfil their ambitions, to the loss of SBI.

One can write huge volumes on the quality of correspondence exchanged between various offices. The Bank was required by law to use Hindi to the maximum extent in correspondence. In fact, officers in most states, South of the

Vindhyas would get away with printing their signature in Hindi, on a letter written in chaste English, treating this as total compliance. The real fun would come when Parliamentary Committees on Implementation of Hindi came visiting. Since conversation in Hindi was compulsory, the strained accent of most would put even Mehmood's spoof of Tamil or Telugu to shame. The officials from South had a very superior attitude and would brag about their prowess in English.

The clash of linguistic cultures often led to peculiar situations. Some were deadly serious. When a South Indian BM reported that the customer had deceased, the Controlling office promptly advised him to complete all formalities to safeguard bank's interests by contacting the deceased borrower. In another hilarious incident, one BM sought for permission to engage a gardener to clean up the premises as there were lots of incest in the grass. Credit proposals often had the recommendation: The proposal is a fair banking risk. If you approve we may decline kindly approve. The sanctioning officer was at a loss as to how to treat this recommendation.

The ubiquitous LUNCH break in SBI is the subject of folklore. It was said that during lunch hours, even the Swiggy delivery boy bringing lunch for the staff wouldn't be allowed in. Bank robbers were totally frustrated because they chose the lunch break to attempt a heist. Despite several reorganization and restructuring attempts, the Lunch break couldn't be tampered with. This break also provided the time for serious investors among the staff to flock to the Local Stock Exchange, especially in metropolitan cities.

It is said that apart from a bus conductor or train ticket examiner, a banker would have interacted with the maximum number of individuals of all hues and shades. This gave him / her the ability to (man/woman)handle the customers with the dexterity and speed of a Roger Federer serve or a Virat Kohli sixer. The experience stood in good stead when handling their assignments on the field and also in the Corporate Hierarchy.

An organisation of this size always needed a separate department to manage its employees. Back then, the Department was known as the Personnel Department. With the winds of change blowing across the world, political correctness crept in. Managing people became Human Relations Management. Name Boards were changed but the people remained the same. The decisions arrived at managed to offend almost everyone across the board. The rules regarding postings at various places were so complex that eventually a solution was found that the family could reside in one place while the employee moved to various assignments. While this assured the family of some stability, it played hell on the personal lives and led to discord and resultant health issues. It is good that no one has compared the medical reimbursement costs with the transfer policies in place. A few examples of HR describe the scenario in a nutshell:

The BM of a remote branch afflicted with Covid was sanctioned leave and simultaneously asked to explain as to how she got herself infected and why didn't she take adequate precautions. Her medical bill was returned twice citing the reason that vaccination was not taken in time, when there was no rule requiring one to do so.

Another employee's traveling expenses bill of nearly Rs.1000 was declined because a bus ticket costing Rs.1.20 was not enclosed.

A third employee who requested for a transfer to take care of his aged parents, got an interesting reply: "At your age, you cannot have parents who are young".

One could go on but the overall message was clear.

SBI has since come a long way with adoption of strong technology. However, in the initial stages, it was a very tough task to make the seasoned veterans abandon pen and paper and adopt the keyboard. Full marks to these pioneers who quickly embraced the technology, once it became clear that the mundane tasks would be eliminated. They became so good at it that in the short space of a year, they became better than the regular techies in the private sector, helped in no small measure by the superior technology available.

Nuts aka Nutrajan and Veda, his demure spouse, were visiting the City of Joy, after a long time, to attend a wedding in the family. They had been booked in a tony club in an ancient building, with high ceilings, rafters of wood, doors through which elephants could enter and a creaking noisy lift. It was staffed with stiff necked waiters headed by a snooty manager, who behaved as if talking to this simple couple was well below his dignity.

The patrons, landing in stretch limos, were completely in sync with the overall atmosphere, dressed in expensive formals and the better half, almost dripping with precious jewellery. The atmosphere was so awe inspiring that the couple tipped the boys (boys?) with 100 rupee notes, which they thought was outrageous, but the waiters seemed to sneer at disdainfully. At dinner, they found that the club, as a rule, did not allow children below 12. Did the patrons come into this world as fully dressed adults and adorned with jewellery? A mischievous thought occurred to both: how did their mothers carry a suited and booted man or a bedecked woman in their wombs? They broke into a wide smile at the incongruity of it all.

Their allotted room was huge, with an ante-room, the furniture all polished teak, topped with marble, the cushions held an old worldly charm and the mattress on the bed was made of coirfoam, which was a great relief for their creaking backs. Having stayed in well-known hotels, their experience was usually depressing. The mattress on the bed was so soft that when one fell on it, it enveloped them in a cocoon as soft as an illegal, stealthy and warm embrace, but one from which they couldn't just get up or out of. The room, outrageously priced, was a tiny cubicle, with a bath with transparent glass walls, leaving nothing to the imagination.

The maximum impression on Nuts was made by a full length mirror on the wardrobe. He had one at home installed in Veda's room, which was forbidden territory. Nuts was seeing his reflection in a full length mirror after maybe a few decades. Grabbing the opportunity with full body, hands proving inadequate, he stared at his whole body scan image. He saw a portly gentleman, with a protruding paunch, a face creased in wrinkles (maybe his thoughts?). He could also see his toes, without having to bend.

Wow, what had happened to the young, dashing, street-smart youngster, which he thought he still was? What about the angry student who had broken a few heads in brawls? What happened to the dashing youngster who had flirted with many a sweet heart in the flush of youth? Where was the young officer who had beaten up rowdy elements in the workplace and killed poisonous snakes with equal toughness? With an agonizing scream, he yelled "Oh God, what has happened to me? Who is this stranger?"

His screams brought Veda, his spouse, into the room. Well past the age of blushing, her first worry was that Nuts had some severe health issues. Once she was reassured on this count by an embarrassed Nuts, Veda being a psychologist par excellence, albeit without any professional training, soothed his nerves and with a gentle prod, asked him to peep behind the reflection. Picking up his scattered modesty, Nuts had a great Surprise. What he saw through his third eye, was a series of reflections, one behind the other, in sequence.

The smallest figure at the back was one he easily recognised. It was a five year old boy, with a scowl on his face, holding a stone, ready to be used as a weapon. He recalled that he had become really angry when his dad refused him permission for a school excursion, which was not affordable. With a lot of patience and understanding, his dad had pacified him. Reluctantly, he went to school but when his classmate taunted him, he took his tiffin box and broke that boy's head. Later they became good friends, but the scar was a permanent one.

Smiling softly at the memory, he could next see a boy of around 12 years, in half pants, playing cricket with a coconut palm frond, with friends, under a jamun tree (blackberry), with a few rags rolled around a piece of wood as a ball. Imagining that they were great cricketers, the matches were played with true ferocity. Adding to the atmosphere, the tree was laden with luscious dark blue and juicy jamuns, which could be gathered by a simple shake of a branch. Mouths stuffed with jamuns, the purple juices splattered all over their dresses, the boys had a marvellous time. When his mom had called these children inside, for a tasty snack of bhajias, it was manna from heaven. Just thinking about these brought out the saliva from his mouth and he started drooling. Veda rushed in. Was he having a relapse or even a stroke? When he sheepishly explained the reason, it was Veda's turn to start drooling.

He recalled with a shudder, the day when news came of his dad being involved in a road mishap. Rushing to a huge hospital with his mother, he saw his dad totally unconscious, swathed in bandages. He saw him subsequently shifting to another hospital sponsored by his father's employer. These events and an extremely slow recovery process were deeply etched in his memory. He also saw that various strangers helped his mother in these difficult times. He also remembered that he suddenly became the man of the house, buying provisions stealthily from vendors who kept the wheels of society moving in times of curfews, walking 8 kms when buses stopped, taking care of the house and even taking up simple cooking. These experiences taught him the values of building societal bonds and helping people without any quid pro quo.

A smart boy of about 18 was waiting next. With a barely visible moustache, he was standing in line for a college admission for an undergraduate course in Science. Unlike the present, seats were available based on individual performance. His parents, especially his father, refused to accompany him to his chosen college. He got admitted, based on his personal interview and his prowess as a player of tenniquoit, which was a game akin to badminton, but played with a heavy rubber ring. He graduated with reasonable scores and also represented his University at State level competitions.

He remembered wryly that the college had an apt moniker Nuisance College. It was adjacent to an equally notorious women's college. Those were turbulent times indeed. Prodded by wily politicians, the gullible student community was up in arms with demands for a separate linguistic state. Agitations and stone throwing were the order of the day. Both boys and girls mingled freely, and participated in agitations and amorous activities with equal gusto. This was the time when glass windows of buses were broken, along with the youngsters' hearts. However, as the old saying goes "this time too shall pass". And so it did.

He next saw a young boy of 21, fresh from college, standing in front of an Interview Board for a job in a big bank. With the naivete of youth, his performance was quite cheeky and done as a lark. However, the interviewers, probably because of a lack of choice, decided to offer him a job. While his dad never said a word, dark clouds were hovering over the family, as he was about to retire and the future was uncertain. The job came in handy and it was made sweeter when his first take-home salary was almost the same as his dad's last drawn salary. He saw that in the relay race called life, at least the baton had been passed on successfully.

A vaguely familiar figure was waiting for him next. He was shocked to see that while it was one person, it had two heads. The body was also dissipated as if no one had cared for it over the passage of time. The first head was that of a snarling wolf in formals, barking and howling, and being the epitome of a disciplinary martinet. The second head was that of a meek and docile individual, trying to fulfil normal familial duties, and always feeling inadequate to the task. With a start, he realised that the cost of simultaneous success at the workplace and home, had taken a great toll on his physique as well as his psyche. This dual personality was the bane of every individual, man or woman, who tried to excel in the role of a juggler, balancing various acts and expecting an applause. Little did one realise that the entire audience was full of jugglers, going through the same activities, seizing opportunities, and trying to LIVE.

With a start, he shook himself up and looked again at the mirror. He saw that his sweet wife was standing beside him and the two images were almost inseparable. This was reality. While appearances changed over the years, the bonds always strengthened with the passage of time. Personal habits got synchronised and attitudes became moderated to accommodate each other. With children having set up their own nest, what remained was the sweet payasam, (kheer) made to perfection with time, to be enjoyed by them.

With a start, both realised that it was time to leave for the wedding. Tradition demanded that on festive occasions and rituals, the men wore their dhoties as panchakacham and the ladies the 9 yards silk saree as madisar. This was a strenuous activity in itself, involving a lot of back bending coordination. Not surprisingly, it was usual for the couple to help each other in getting this to perfection. Resplendent in their attire, the happy couple enjoyed the wedding and showered their blessings on the happy young couple, of course, accompanied by an expensive gift. After a hearty lunch, and with the warm glow of a day well spent, they returned back to their room.

On a lazy summer afternoon, Nuts and Veda, after lunch, were dozing in their house, located in Triplicane, one of the busiest localities in Chennai where the roads were crowded throughout the year. They had just completed making sweets and savouries for Krishna Jayanthi. Towards the end of a sweltering summer, while real rains played truant, it was raining discounts in all shops, from shoes, to jewellery, to garments and even idli/dosa batter. Nature did its best to join the party and in Chennai the winds, whatever little was there, also brought in super fine dust"free".

This was also the season of the beginning of various festivals. The Gods, especially Lord Ganesha and Lord Krishna had their birthdays within a fortnight. Both were quite mischievous babies and loved the good life. Sweets, savouries, milk, butter, ghee and all sorts of delicious offerings were made as offerings to these charming divine babies. In all households, the families began preparations at least a week in advance. The provision vendors did roaring business. Keeping in view the changing times, most items were being sold in pre-mix form. Cooking was made simple by preparing the pre-mix as instructed, and then frying or baking or pressure - cooking the item, as instructed by YouTube Master chefs.

As if in a trance, Nuts and Veda could hear the mellifluous notes on a flute and the heavy rhythmic sounds of percussion. They saw Krishna with his flute and Ganesha, chomping on a cane, banging away on his mridangam, moving in the skies. It was quite evident that they were conducting an aerial survey of their own birthday celebrations, which were within a few days of each other. As befitting the modern world, Krishna was astride an eagle shaped drone named Garudan while Ganesha, was doing his best to settle his gargantuan frame comfortably on the mouse shaped drone aptly-named Mooshika. As both drones were capable of time travel, they decided to enjoy their birthdays, once again.

As Krishna's birthday was first, it was time to enjoy the Krishna Janmashtami celebrations. Ganesha was looking at the various sweets and savouries laid out in the welcome of Krishna in each household.

From tasty crispies like cheedai, murukku of various types, laddus, Mysore Pak, appams and sugiyan, the offerings included cupfuls of butter, milk jars, ghee and to top it all, jaggery mixed with dry ginger, as a digestive. Ganesha told Krishna that with a single whoop of his trunk, all the sweets would vanish in a blink. He asked Krishna as to how could he ever finish all the offerings within a single evening. He was also intrigued by the huge amounts of butter and milk. Jokingly he told Krishna that all this would adversely impact his weight loss program. Krishna, with a knowing look, told Ganesha that if the entire Universe could be within his mouth as seen by Yashoda, partaking of such foods was literally child's play for him.

Ganesha was also enjoying the way Baby Krishna was being welcomed in each house, with small baby footsteps drawn in Rangoli. It was Krishna's turn to tease Ganesha about his huge footprints which could never fit in most of the houses. Moreover, who would like a baby elephant in the house when in all probability, the baby would run riot. Ganesha quietly emphasised that a baby elephant was one of the cutest of God's creations and was far more intelligent than any other living being. Wasn't a strong ability to store and recollect knowledge called an Elephantine Memory?

Moving on, they saw various ways of celebrating Krishna's birthday. In a re-enactment of his butter and curd stealing ways, these items were strung high along with a pot of valuable goodies too, which was sought to be taken by forming a human pyramid. Called Dahi handi, Uri Adi and in many other names, it was an exciting adventure sport for the youth. The winner collected the prize which was shared and the losers collected many bruises at best and a few broken bones in the worst case scenario.

There were many who liked to gamble at the first opportunity. Be it Janmashtami or Diwali, any festival was an excuse for this all-time favourite. Apparently Lord

Krishna was known to play Chausar or dice with friends and family. The game could also have symbolized victory of good over evil. Could it also have been a throwback on the gambling episode in Mahabharata? One never could be sure.

There were many childrens' costume parties. Babies dressed as Krishna and Radha jutted around the stage in their new clothes. Children being children, Krishna and Radha would occasionally get into a whacking fight with their cute flutes and dandias. Bawling away, they would go to their mothers, who would escalate the fight to the next level. Ganesha and Krishna could not but laugh when they saw the two children, scared from the violent fighting between their mothers, running away, hand in hand, giggling happily and stealing their favourite sweets from the offerings, while their mothers were competing for the WWF Championship title.

To top it all, and in keeping with the principle of Unity in Diversity, Krishna Janmashtami was celebrated by different sects on succeeding dates. Most times, the festivities were spread over three days. Thus, Krishna, through his devotees, could enjoy sequential birthdays with all goodies at his leisure.

It was time for Krishna and Ganesha to survey Ganesha's birthday. A few days before the festival, all streets in the city were filled with idols of the elephant God, in all sizes and exotic shapes too. Clay, plaster of Paris and many other materials were used, with emphasis on their being eco-friendly. Since families couldn't afford to have a lively elephant in their average one / two BHK apartment, traditions warranted that Ganesha idols be installed in each home. Adorned with beautiful decorations, the house itself had a divine look.

The offerings included sweet modakams (dumplings made from rice dough stuffed with grated coconut and jaggery) salted modakams, sundal, besides the usual feast associated with festivals, which over time, morphed into fe(a)stivals. Krishna asked Ganesha if he wasn't bored with the lack of variety in his offerings. Ganesha, with a twinkle in his small eyes, said that while variety may be the spice of life, his gargantuan appetite would only be filled with huge quantities of Modakams, which were his staple diet. Also, the cheedais and murukkus and appams would vanish without a trace even before he could get the taste and flavour of each item.

About a century ago, the practice of celebrating Ganesha's birthday as a community was started. Taking clue from the Olympic Motto of CITIUS, ALTIUS, FORTIUS translated as faster, higher and stronger, the idols of Ganesha grew in size from year to year. These public celebrations lasted nearly a fortnight before the idols got immersed in the sea or nearest water body. The economic activities surrounding these celebrations were hugely successful too. When Krishna asked Ganesha as to how he felt when after the celebrations, the idols were immersed in water, Ganesha reminded Krishna that this simply reflected the eternal philosophy of life cycles.

Both Gods being extremely perceptive, had observed that during their birthdays, most families made only traditional dishes. It was as if they were trying to re-create their ancestral way of life. A more practical reason was that such traditional eats, loved by everyone, were quite difficult to make and hence could be reserved for festive occasions only.

Both Krishna and Ganesha decided to have some fun. They popped into Nuts and Veda's puja room and decided to eat up the offerings. While Krishna swallowed the jar of butter, Ganesha, with a single intake of breath, gulped away almost all the sweets and savouries through his trunk. In their trance, the couple gasped at the sight of the empty serving dishes. They simply couldn't understand who had eaten away all their offerings. Wonderstruck, they thought that the children of the neighborhood had come in and helped themselves. After their daughter had got married, they had become the go-to pseudo grandparents of many neighborhood children, whose parents were working and lived in the cocoon of nuclear families.

At this moment, a small inner voice told them that it was We who had taken the offerings given by you. Not able to believe, they remonstrated that if the

Lords ate everything, then what would be left for their devotees and themselves? And therein, friends, lay the simple truth. All offerings to the Lord were meant to be distributed amongst the devotees. In today's materialistic world, the day any Lord decided to consume everything on offer, the offerings would dry up.
Nuts and Veda, woke with a start to find their offerings intact. Still unable to come to terms with their strange dream, they began preparations for the evening celebrations to welcome Baby Krishna, in the company of the neighborhood kids.

Ganesha and Krishna, after having had their Babys' day out, returned to their celestial abode, with a promise to their devotees that they would be back next year.

==============================

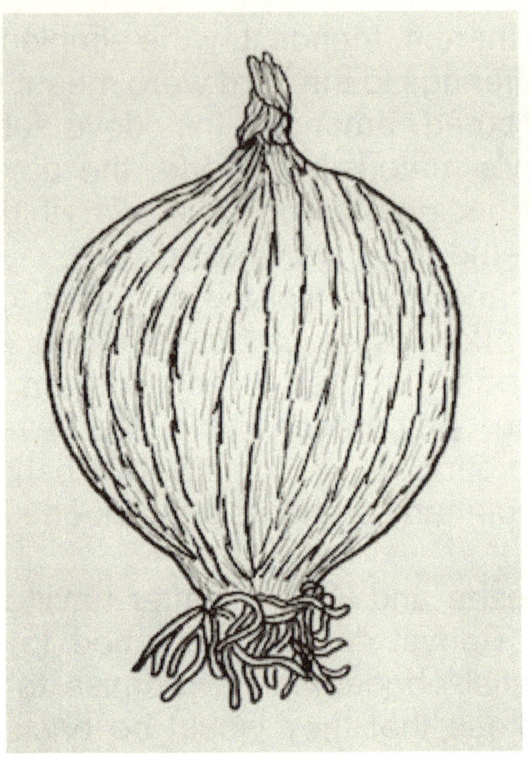

It was the busy and enjoyable season of Navaratri festival again. Nuts (aka Nutrajan) and Veda had continued the delightful tradition of setting up their modest Golu (exhibition of toys and dolls) at home, with collections from all over the world. Inviting guests for the traditional haldi kumkum ceremonies each evening, praying to the various forms of Devi, the celestial mother and visiting friends and relatives were an integral part of the celebrations. By the end of the day, both were tired to the core and would promptly fall asleep, without help of any tranquillisers.

Waking up early one morning, Veda thought she heard someone crying softly. The sounds were coming from her kitchen larder. Alarmed at this unusual activity, she, being a brave lady, went into the kitchen and switched on the lights. The sounds had stopped immediately. At first, she couldn't understand or see anything or anyone. Having heard the strange noises clearly, she started peering into the shelves for storage, although how one could hide there was a big question. The builders who had sold her the flat had cut so many corners while constructing the flat that all that remained was only corners. The rooms were tiny, kitchens even more so and bathrooms were modelled on the solitary confinement rooms of high security prisons, where one could neither stand nor sit.

Veda suddenly stepped on a small pool of water near a shelf. Upon closer looks, she found that there was a single Onion in the tray, crying softly and shedding tears. Startled that a vegetable could have such strong emotions, and being inquisitive, as most seenagers (elders with a young heart) usually are, she started asking the Onion the reason for her misery. The story unravelled as the Onion opened her heart out to a sympathetic Veda.

“We Onions came from an illustrious and prosperous family lineage, tracing their ancestors to Central Asia. They were well known to the global population, and were likely first eaten long before the invention of writing or farming. Onions were also one of the earliest cultivated crops because they were easy to grow, transportable, less perishable and could be grown in a variety of climates and soils. Because of their widespread popularity, Onions became a global favourite, and were treated lavishly by the royalty and commoners alike. Known for their flavour, health benefits, and medicinal properties, they held an exalted position in the hierarchy of foods. They also had esoteric uses in rituals, black magic and arts."

Veda was excited to know that the humble Onion had such an interesting history. She was also surprised at the Onion's behaviour. Her question was answered with a fresh bout of tears.

"Look at me, just look at me", the Onion wailed. "I am all alone, a single piece on this tray, and no one has even had a look at me for the past one month. I am extremely lonely with not even another Onion to give me company. I understand from my WhatsApp group colleagues that all of them are facing a social boycott. There is no one to care for them. The farmers are unable to sell their produce because of a sharp fall in demand. When eating out, the customers are asking for food without Onions and Garlic. Is this the way you thankless humans treat a friend who has been with you as an inseparable part of your life?"

"We Onions add flavour and spice to whatever you cook in the kitchen. Even a novice can become an expert in the culinary arts, by knowing how and when to add Onions to a special dish. We give real meaning to the old proverb 'the way to a person's heart is through the stomach.' Our taste is unique. Foods flavoured with Onions are also known to be mood enhancers, and kindle the romantic spirits by acting as aphrodisiacs. Our juices are also capable of acting as an antidote to poisonous bites from the creepy crawlies. We are simply unable to come to terms with your behaviour in completely avoiding us and literally insulting us. Is this how friends behave?"

Slowly, Veda started to understand the problem. It was the season of Shradh Paksha or Mahalaya. It was the time, when for a fortnight, each family would pay obeisance to their departed ancestors by conducting pujas and rituals to propitiate their souls. The feast served to our ancestors was entirely Sattvik in nature, in keeping with their status of having become one with the Gods. Traditionally, it was the time for the family also to abstain from foods which were classified as Tamasic in nature, which could, if consumed lead one astray from the path of devotion and prayers. All flavour enhancers were usually in this category. It was the time for persons to "Eat to Live" rather than "Live to Eat". This period of austerity was immediately followed by the sacred Navaratras, wherein also, the prasad and food preparations were entirely Sattvik in nature, in keeping with the dignity of the occasion. It was no wonder that in India, therefore, Onions and their ilk like garlic, were not consumed in this period.

Veda gave the Onion a comforting pat on the back and explained the situation in simple terms. She pointed out that this phenomenon was confined to India only and the rest of the World was comfortable with Onions and Garlic. It was also the time for Onions to conserve their potency and increase the strength of the inherent sulphurous compounds, which is what gave them the ability to add flavour to the foods and add zest to the common man's life. They could also take revenge by making people cry more, when cutting up such potent Onions. Moreover, the sacred period is almost getting over and the demand for Onions has already started increasing as witnessed by the sharp rise in market prices in the past few days. Onions are so powerful that increases in their price could have far reaching consequences including falling of Governments.

With a smile on her face, Veda couldn't resist a parting shot: "My dear Onion, today you are crying but the day is not far off when you will regain your throne in the culinary space. Then you can have your sweet revenge by making everyone cry, whenever they cut an Onion. To twist an old saying":

"EVERY ONION HAS ITS DAY"

Leading a well-deserved retired life, Nuts aka Nutrajan and Veda, the quintessential Tambrahm couple were living peacefully in the bylanes surrounding the Parthasarathy Temple in Chennai. Having had a hectic life, loitering all over the country thanks to his employers, they had experienced the four traditional seasons of Spring,

Summer, Autumn and Winter, in all their splendor. They had realised a long time back that these seasons also represented various phases of Life, beginning with Spring, growing with Summer, resting in Autumn and winding up in Winter. It was up to the person to appreciate these, based on his or her frame of mind.

Each season brought it's share of Festivals, to celebrate the joy of living and celebrating it with one's near and dear, almost always ending in a gastronomic extravaganza, so much so that most festivals had transmogrified into FE(A)STIVALS.

Nuts and Veda, were no exception to celebrating such festivals with gusto. While Nuts was the foodie, Veda was the baddie who restricted the foodie from over indulgence. Since they had traversed across different states, their knowledge of the goodies made in each state's festival was quite good. However, with advancing age, doctors had diagnosed them as borderline diabetic.

In other words, sugar, fats, fried delicacies and other rich tasty foods were restricted. In its place, bitter gourd juice, soups made from unrecognisable greens which made one go green in the face, strange millet dishes which were the current rage, due to celebrity endorsements and very limited quantities of coffee, that heavenly nectar, invariably graced the d(wh)ining table. To top it all, a dash of religious fervour ensured that for at least half the month, many delicacies were restricted for consumption. Fridays,Tuesdays, Thursdays, Ekadashi, Dwadashi, Amavasya and many such days ensured that both the sugar borderline and waistline remained in control.

Nuts and Veda were quite fond of traveling and visiting temples. Their experience in many famous temples were not very great, to say the least. To begin with, the temples of S India, built by the kings and queens, were on a massive scale. The distance from the main entrance to the sanctum sanctorum made for a healthy walk. The doorsteps in each level were at least one foot high, built with massive stones. It was tradition that one should not step on this while entering the temple. However, with the current generation being inflicted with all sorts of health issues, and being weak kneed (in all senses of the term), it was almost impossible to make the leap of faith.

Once in, the queues stretched endlessly. People who could pay well, had special privileges. Even in payment, there were different grades. The common devotee could but gaze helplessly while the well-heeled breezed past their queue, waving wads of special tickets. A wad of currency notes, if held visibly, could be the grease in the palm, and ensure even better treatment. After all the pushing and shoving endured in the queues, one could barely have a glimpse of the deity, maybe for a few seconds. The security would simply shove you out of the queue and if they were not able to do so, the crowd would ensure that you are thrown out unceremoniously. The overwhelming feeling was that it was only staunch devotion which kept the devotees braving the crowds to pay obeisance to the Lord. Having braved the crowds and visited such important temples, Nuts and Veda had the feeling that with advancing age, visits to such temples could reduce, if not altogether stop, to avoid collateral damages to the body. After all, the Soul, blessed by the darshan of the Lord, had to still reside in the physical body which He had allotted.

The relatively unknown temples, which were also in their itinerary, were a study in contrast. Every village or small town boasted of its own temple with a long history. Ancient texts had meticulously listed out the temples and their deities. Most were built by the ruling kings and chieftains in these parts. These temples were as big, if not bigger than their famous counterparts. The distance from the entrance to the sanctum sanctorum, the height of steps, the massive doorways were all similar. What was missing was the devotees, the ceremonial splendor and gaiety. In many temples, after the morning ritual puja, the temples had a haunted look. One was scared to walk alone in the towering precincts, with crumbling walls and high ceiling where birds and bats ruled. Many smaller temples were barely able to afford to light a few auspicious lamps in the sanctum sanctorum. The priests (usually one or two only) would carry on their work, with barely any hope of eking out a decent living. The prasadam offered to the Gods was of very poor quality. Maybe that's why, Gods had decided to feast with their eyes only. In a lighter vein, if the Gods began eating the offerings of prasadam, would anyone offer these in future? Nuts and Veda had visited a large number of such temples and were happy to contribute their mite to lighting a few lamps in these temples, offer prasad and promise to send whatever they could towards their upkeep. With pleasant thoughts floating in their minds, they also had the opportunity to visit a few of the ancient ashrams which abounded in and around these ancient temples.

Most temples, big or small, had dedicated religious ashrams attached to them. These were better endowed than the temple itself, with properties in their name, or in the name of the temple, donated by devotees, which yielded decent income. With time, these assets became valuable. Today, the situation is that there are very few persons willing to serve the deities in the temple as pujaris, but there are many legal tussles in courts to head these ashrams. After paying obeisance in these mutts, Nuts and Veda observed a strange phenomenon: there were more visitors to these mutts than to the temples, probably proving the hoary saying: Guru is the path to the Gods.

To cater to the aspirations and needs of the current generation, well-educated and needing support in view of growing social insecurities, the philosophers and savants of the modern world have had to adopt a radically different approach. The world is looking up to India to imbibe and benefit from practicing Yoga, taking ayurvedic treatments, joining nature food camps and meditation camps and learning ancient dance forms. As Global citizens they, however, expect the comforts and luxuries which are ingrained in their daily routines. Today's ashrams, meditation centres and the like are being built in vast swathes of verdant jungle spaces, far away from the hustle and bustle of metros. Rivulets flow serenely, cows graze peacefully, agriculture and other activities flourish in these areas. These are self-contained islands of luxury and excellence. The approach roads would put any metro city road to shame. There are helipads, accommodations rivalling the best 7 star hotels, restaurants which would make Michelin starred ones blush and other such conveniences, to ease the discomfort faced during the course of the recuperation cum treatment. With huge statues of the divine, and vast open spaces for celebration of festivals en masse, these wonderlands have become star attractions in their own right. It was quite normal for the super-rich to indulge around the globe and come here for detox at an exorbitant price. A win-win business proposition, if ever there was one.

Social media has played a significant role in bringing out the benefits of ancient Indian wisdom to the masses. The gurus and swamis range across the spectrum from superstars to humble saints next door. The world's largest University is now the Internet, with WhatsApp being the most reputed institution in this world. The (mis)information shared by all and sundry is humongous. With Life's insecurities mounting exponentially, such information gains attention of those who think it's an answer to their prayers. The reputation of the philosophers and spiritual guides has soared beyond imagination. The mental wellness industry is one of the fastest growing industries in the world, with allied benefits of commercial development.

Nuts and Veda had the opportunity to visit a few of these places as well, both as tourists and in one case, as participants. It was awe-inspiring to say the least. Of course, there were many places which also offered simplistic living style, traditional treatments and a disciplined way of life, in stark contrast to the above, since there was a growing awareness and therefore, the need to modify lifestyles to improve the quality of life. Nuts and Veda had spent a fortnight in one such retreat, and came out with glowing skins and almost empty wallets.

Apparently, the rulers of the past had built huge temples and other religious structures as places where people could meet without barriers, since other entertainment avenues were non-existent. The building of such structures also provided direct employment to the population. These places were also used to store good quality seedlings for raising crops, in case of any natural disaster. Nuts and Veda, while visiting these places, had realised that these ancient temples and their modern-day incarnation of huge congregations had come full circle to satisfy the social needs of the growing population. Just as humans had evolved from lower forms, the social infrastructure had also evolved over time and was quite competent in catering to the needs of society, thirsting for experiences to improve their lifestyle.

With these thoughts, Nuts and Veda began packing their bags for their next trip.

=====================

A conversation on the prevalence of cataract in the elderly, led me to describe my own experiences in this regard.

"I was fifteen, going on sixteen,
Winking at everyone.
Not knowing that I always,
Had a blurred vision.

One day my daddy, Caught me winking,
And realised clearly, that I was blinking.
He asked me to read a film poster,
Which, I couldn't read between.

He promptly hauled me to the doc,
Who put him in the dock,
For having failed to see,
That his son just couldn't see.

My dad was proud, though,
That like Tendulkar in his first (eye)
Test,
His son had hit a sixer (-6.5)
Which he never could.

Ever since, I've had glasses, Not with sparkling wine,
But to see the dishes, Whenever I dine.

Now on 66, going on 67, I visit the doc annually.
Despite his best efforts, to cut my eyes,
I still manage to see.

The doc feels cheated, but I feel elated,
How things have worked out,
I'm now able to wink at girls freely,

Without creating any doubt.

Privileges of a Seenager !!!

www.ingramcontent.com/pod-product-compliance
Lightning Source LLC
LaVergne TN
LVHW041105150826
845673LV00007B/1937

* 9 7 9 8 8 9 6 3 2 1 9 3 4 *